POKÉMON

4EVER

The Voice of t[he Forest]

Movie Adaptation by
Howie Dewin

SCHOLASTIC INC.
New York   Toronto   London   Auckland   Sydney
Mexico City   New Delhi   Hong Kong   Buenos Aires

Contents

Prologue

The Voice of the Forest

Whoosh! A small green, wide-eyed Pokémon darted through the air of a beautiful ancient forest deep in the Johto region. The Pokémon called Celebi was an excellent and fast flyer. But it still couldn't shake Houndoom, the vicious doglike Pokémon chasing it.

As it flew for its life, it whizzed by the head of a young boy walking through the forest. The boy barely had time to react before Houndoom raced by and nearly trampled him.

The boy quickly followed the chase. A serious Pokémon trainer, he might have been a friend of Ash Ketchum's except he

1

was from a different time. He wore old-styled clothing and an outdated hairstyle. But that didn't stop him from running after the curious little green Pokémon in trouble. He approached an enormous tree trunk lying on its side with a passage cut through the trunk. This was the entrance to the very heart of the forest.

"If you're going in," called out a pleasant voice, "be careful!"

The boy stopped. He turned and saw a young woman in a long dress and old-fashioned hat. She stepped gracefully down the huge trunk to greet him.

"Don't forget," the girl continued, "if you hear the voice of the forest, don't move a muscle."

"What's the voice of the forest?" the young boy asked.

"They say there's a sound you can hear when the spirit that protects the forest is time traveling." She spoke slowly and earnestly.

"Time traveling?" the boy asked in disbelief.

"That's one of its special powers," the

girl answered. "It can go back and forth be-tween the past and the future."

"Wow," the boy uttered.

"So if you hear a weird sound," she warned, "stop and stay completely still. . . . If the spirit catches you it could carry you off to a different time."

"I'll be careful," the boy declared and hur-ried toward the passage into the deep forest.

"Wait," the girl ran after him. She handed him a loaf of bread. "It's full of berries from the forest and it might come in handy if you get hungry."

"Thanks," the boy said as he took the bread. "I appreciate it."

While the boy was talking to the young girl, Celebi's attackers had increased in number. A very nasty Scyther — a Grass Pokémon — had joined the Houndoom in the hunt. The sweet-natured green Poké-mon was losing ground. It looked like Celebi could not get away.

Suddenly, a Pokémon Hunter approached on a motorcycle. He laughed a wicked laugh. "You've been givin' me the slip for a long time," the Hunter hissed at Celebi. "But you won't today!" The Hunter pulled out a Poké Ball and threw it at Celebi. Though it was exhausted, Celebi reacted quickly. It surrounded itself with a protective orb that ricocheted the Poké Ball. Celebi then zipped away through the trees.

The chase continued. Once again, the young boy found himself directly in their path. This time he wouldn't lose them! He took off at a full run. He had to protect the little Pokémon.

The boy caught up with the Hunter and his Pokémon just in time. They had managed to corner Celebi, who lay panting on the ground.

"Let it go!" the boy shouted. "Two against one isn't a fair fight!"

Celebi took advantage of the moment and blasted the Scyther and Houndoom with a tangle of vine. The boy quickly swooped in and grabbed the Celebi.

"Hand over the Celebi," the Hunter boomed.

"Why should I?" the boy retorted.

"I'm a Pokémon Hunter, kid! I make good money off of rare Pokémon. I catch 'em and auction them off to the highest bidder."

"Not this Pokémon!" the boy snapped.

"Give it to me," the Hunter insisted. But the boy took off through the forest. He held tight to the rare and terrified Pokémon.

He ran as fast as he could, but the Hunter's motorcycle was faster. Suddenly a strange sound surrounded him and a shock of white light filled the air.

The young girl at the entrance to the forest looked up toward the sky.

Deep in the forest, the boy stumbled. He and the Celebi disappeared before he hit the ground.

Forty Years Later . . .

An old man stood outside a run-down cabin in that same forest. He was an old Pokémon Hunter tending the many caged Pokémon surrounding his cabin.

Suddenly, a large hulking man wearing a mask over half his face appeared before the old hunter. "I'm here because I heard a story that you almost caught a Celebi somewhere in this forest about forty years ago," he growled.

"I'm still a Pokémon Hunter," the old man replied. "I'm not telling you."

"We'll see about that," the scary stranger answered. He pulled out a black Poké Ball.

"What's that?" the Hunter asked nervously.

"A Dark Ball," the masked man answered. "The Pokémon I catch with the Dark Ball become evil Pokémon, and their power instantly increases to the highest level!"

Iron Mask laughed and threw the Dark Ball into the air. "Come on out, Tyranitar!" he shouted.

The Poké Ball released an enormous Tyranitar that began destroying things almost before it was visible. It turned in each direction and shot enormous fire blasts. Within seconds, the hunter's entire camp was burning.

"No, please!" the Hunter begged. "It's gonna destroy everything! I'll show you! I'll show you the spot where I found that Celebi!"

Iron Mask threw back his head and laughed. The sound he made was pure evil.

Chapter One

The Legend of Suicune

In a small old seaside village, Ash, Misty, Brock, and Pikachu were about to travel to a new Pokémon gym in the Johto League. Brock and Misty stood on the dock waiting for Ash and Pikachu.

"If they don't come soon they're gonna miss the boat!" Misty exclaimed. She scanned the village looking for Ash and his little Electric Pokémon.

"Crobat, go!" commanded Brock. He threw a Poké Ball into the air. A flying Pokémon appeared and headed off in search of Ash.

It found him quickly. Ash and Pikachu were in the middle of a challenge with a local trainer. But when Ash saw Crobat, he realized he had forgotten to check the time. He quickly ran to the ferry. It was just about to leave the dock.

"Pikachu, let's go!" he shouted.

Ash ran as fast as he could, while Misty and Brock stood anxiously on the deck of the boat. The boat moved from the dock just as Ash and Pikachu arrived. Ash held tight to Pikachu and took a flying leap toward the ferry. Brock reached out his hands, but they missed each other. Ash and Pikachu were just about to fall into the water below, when another hand reached out. A good-looking teenage boy pulled them safely aboard the ferry.

Ash sputtered and fought to catch his breath before he thanked the man for his help. The man introduced himself as White. Ash began to explain why he had been late by telling them about his Pokémon battles.

"Sounds like you're interested in Pokémon," White smiled.

"Yeah!" Ash confirmed.

"I come from a place just up the river, and a lot of real unusual Pokémon live in the forest nearby," White told Ash and his friends.

"Maybe we can stop off and check it out!" Ash exclaimed.

"No problem," White offered. "We'll get off at the next stop, and I'll take you the rest of the way in my boat."

"*Pika!*" Pikachu said in gratitude.

As the ferry neared the dock, Pikachu cried out again. Ash turned to see Pikachu pointing toward the lush green forest. There in a mist was a horselike Pokémon with a beautiful flowing mane. It appeared for a second and then moved quickly from view.

"Was that a Pokémon?" Ash asked in amazement.

"Looked like one to me," nodded White. "The woods are full of 'em."

Ash couldn't wait to get into the forest. But first he wanted to check with his mentor Professor Oak about what he'd just seen. When they got off the ferry, he called him and quickly described what he'd seen. Professor Oak listened intently.

"It was Suicune," he said seriously.

"What kind of Pokémon is that?" Brock asked.

"It's one of the legendary Pokémon, Brock, and not very much is known about it. According to folktales, Suicune personifies the North Wind and it's believed to have the power to purify tainted waters."

"Cool!" Ash said. Now he really couldn't wait to get into the forest. He said good-bye to Professor Oak and ran toward White's boat. They sped away up a sparkling blue river that ran through the forest.

High above the sky, a trio of evil but silly villains pedaled a glider madly.

Jessie, James, and Meowth of evil Team Rocket were once again tracking Ash and his friends. They were determined to capture Pikachu.

"Those twerps won't get away now. They're right beneath us," hissed Jessie with her long hair blowing in the wind.

"Of course they're beneath us," snarled James. "They're twerps!"

"All we have to do is swoop in and swipe Pikachu!" screeched Meowth, the talking catlike Pokémon.

Jessie let out a yelp. "Something's wrong with my leg! All this pedaling has given me a cramp!"

Without Jessie's help, the glider began to swerve and drop.

"You can't cramp! We'll crash!" James shouted.

As Team Rocket careened toward the ground, White's boat was in its own trouble.

"What do we do now?" Misty asked nervously as she stared up at an enormous cliff and waterfall shooting straight to the skies. "How do we get up?"

"Don't worry, Misty," White said with a curious smile. "You'll see."

Chapter Two

A Legend and the Truth

White worked the levers and cranks of his boat, and slowly the pontoons lifted from the water. They filled with air, and the boat began to gently lift into the sky. Soon they were gliding above the trees. Ash and his friends were amazed. They leaned over the sides and saw the beauty of the forest below them.

Before long, White smiled and said, "Well, we're here."

"Here?" Ash sputtered. "Where?"

A clearing appeared in the thick forest

growth. Below them was an amazing, multi-leveled tree-house village.

"This is HatenoVille," White announced as he lowered them to the ground.

An enormous log with a passageway cut through it stood before them. Ash jumped out of the boat ready to explore.

"Stop right there!" a stern voice called out. An old lady in a long dress appeared. "I suppose you're heading into the forest to look for Pokémon!"

"Yes, ma'am!" Ash proclaimed.

"Then you're gonna love what you see," said a very pretty young girl who had come up behind the old woman.

"Tell me your name!" Brock said, his eyes wide open in awe.

"My name's Diana and that's my Grandma. She's been guarding the entrance to the forest since she was my age!"

"Listen for the voice of the forest," Towa, the old woman, said calmly. "If you hear it, stop and be still or you won't get away."

"It's an old village legend," added Diana.

"Yes," Towa agreed. "It's a legend and a true one!"

"We gotta hurry," Ash said, "but thanks a lot for the warning! Come on, Pikachu!"

"*Pika!*" Pikachu chirped as they ran toward the forest entrance.

Ash, Misty, and Brock made their way through the passage and headed deep into the forest.

"I wonder what she meant by 'the voice of the forest,'" Brock said quietly. "Maybe the sound of the wind . . . or the trees . . . the water . . . maybe the voices of Pokémon."

Before anyone could respond, the air filled with a straight blue and white light that moved in waves of sound and energy. Ash clung to Pikachu, while Misty held tight to her little Togepi.

"Maybe it's the voice of the forest," Misty shouted.

"That way!" Ash cried as he ran toward the source of the light and sound.

"Shouldn't we stand still?" Brock cried. But it was too late. Ash was gone. Misty and Brock ran to catch him.

They reached a small clearing in the woods just as the strange waves of sound and light disappeared.

"It's a kid," Ash called out.

There on the stone floor of an overgrown old courtyard lay a boy about Ash's age. He was absolutely still.

"He's breathing," Misty exclaimed.

"Let's take him back to Diana's house!" Ash shouted. He hoisted the unconscious boy onto his shoulders. The three friends quickly retraced their steps.

"Diana!" Brock called as they neared the tree house. "We need help!"

Ash laid the boy on the ground, and he began to stir.

"He's waking up," Misty said.

"Take it easy," Ash said. "You're gonna be okay."

Before the boy was even on his feet, he pushed Ash away in a panic.

"What'd you do with that Celebi!" the boy cried out.

"Hey!" shouted Ash. "I'm trying to help!"

The boy looked confused. "Where am I? . . . How'd I get here?"

Diana and Towa came quickly down the ladder from their house.

"What's going on?" Diana asked urgently.

The boy looked blankly at Diana and her grandmother.

Towa took one look at the boy and ran to him. "You've come back," she exclaimed and wrapped her arms around him. "Thank goodness!"

"Grandma," Diana asked slowly, "where did he come back from?"

"I've told you the story about the little boy that disappeared in the forest," Towa said tearfully.

"But this boy can't be him," Diana said.

"But it is," Towa said.

The boy looked at Towa's face.

"You're the girl who gave me the loaf of bread," the boy said slowly.

"Yes," Towa replied.

Chapter Three

Reunited

Everyone sat around an old wooden table in Towa's cabinlike tree-house home. It was a cozy room with a warm light glowing and colorful woven rugs and blankets. But Ash and his friends were too fascinated by the strange boy's story to notice much else.

"I've kept this all these years in case you ever came back," Towa said as she slid an old leather-bound book across the table.

"This is my sketchbook!" the boy exclaimed.

"You've been away for forty years," Towa told him softly.

"The legend says the voice of the forest

can take a person on a trip through time," Diana said.

Ash stared in amazement.

Then, as if he suddenly remembered, the boy snapped to attention. "What happened to Celebi? Was there a Pokémon with me in the forest?" he demanded.

"We didn't see any," Misty answered.

"The Pokémon you met that day was Celebi?" Towa asked excitedly.

The boy nodded.

"We know Celebi as the voice of the forest . . . the spirit that protects it," Towa explained.

"You must have both been in danger, and Celebi picked the fastest way to get out of it," Diana stated, explaining the time travel. "It escaped to the future and took you with it!" Everyone in the room was stunned.

Towa nodded and continued. "Celebi lives deep in the forest at the Lake of Life. That's probably where it's gone now."

"I've got a feeling Celebi may still be hurt," the boy said. "I have to find Celebi."

"I'll go with you!" Ash said without hesitation.

Misty and Brock agreed, and then realized that they hadn't even introduced themselves.

"I'm Brock. I'm a Pokémon breeder."

"I'm Misty. My speciality is Water Pokémon."

"I'm Ash Ketchum. I'm trying to become a Pokémon Master! This is Pikachu."

"*Pika!*" the Pokémon squeaked.

The boy smiled for the first time. "Hi, Pikachu. I'm Sammy."

The new friends thanked Towa and Diana and headed into the forest.

Not far away, Jessie, James, and Meowth had finally landed their flying machine. The trio hung from the branches of a big tree.

"Next time we'll spring for a motor," Meowth said, staring at the wreckage of their glider.

"I wonder where those twerps are," Jessie snapped just as Ash came into his view. "I can't believe my eyes," she whispered.

"Let's get down and tail 'em," Meowth squawked.

Ash and his friends made their way

through the forest when Pikachu suddenly cried out. "*Pikachu!*" The kids immediately stopped. Something strange was happening.

"Look up there!" Ash cried. He pointed to the top of two enormous fallen trees where an unusually large group of Pokémon stood watching something.

Ash took a running leap onto a tree trunk and began climbing it like a monkey. Sammy was right behind him. Ash kept a watchful eye on Sammy as they heaved themselves up toward the gathering of Pokémon. He was afraid Sammy might still be weak. When they finally got to the top, they saw why the Pokémon were gathered.

A weak and frightened Celebi was tucked into a nook of the tree. Sammy went right to it. But Celebi sent out a wave of energy that sent Ash and Sammy flying backward. Sammy immediately tried again.

"Come on, Celebi," he said. But now Celebi lashed out with fast snapping vines. It whipped anything it could reach.

"What'd you do that for?" Ash exclaimed. "We're trying to help!"

"It's afraid and hurt," Sammy said gently. "A hunter attacked it."

"We're your friends," Ash said to the Celebi.

"I tried to help you before," Sammy pleaded. "Don't you remember?" Sammy reached out and tenderly touched the Celebi's head. This time it didn't attack. It closed its eyes, relieved.

"You're safe with me, Celebi," Sammy said. He scooped up the green Pokémon, and he and Ash hurried back to Brock and Misty.

"It seems really weak," Misty exclaimed when she saw Celebi.

"We better hurry!" Brock agreed. "We'll take it to a Pokémon Center!"

They ran through the forest to save Celebi's life.

Before they'd gotten far, a blast of smoke stopped them in their tracks.

When the smoke cleared, Team Rocket was directly above them on a tree branch.

Ash glared at the foolish trio. There was no time for them now! They were nothing but trouble.

Chapter Four

Iron Mask Attacks

Just as Team Rocket was about to lunge for Pikachu, their big blue Wobbuffet Pokémon appeared on the tree branch next to them. The extra weight was just enough to bring the branch crashing down.

Ash and his friends grabbed the opportunity to get away.

"Do you think they're gonna be okay?" Sammy asked, looking back in concern.

"Unfortunately, yes," Misty hissed.

"Hang in there, Celebi," Sammy murmured.

"There's the village up there!" Ash shouted as a towering peak came into view.

But something else came into view, too.

An enormous metal machine with four long, spidery legs stepped out of the forest and blocked the path to the village. High above the long legs sat a control panel run by a hulking man in a mask.

"I've been looking for that Celebi," his voice boomed.

"Who are you?" Ash insisted.

"A Pokémon lover!" Iron Mask growled.

Jessie, James, and Meowth hid behind a tree and watched.

"He's tryin' to steal our Pikachu," Meowth said.

"We won't let him!" James sneered as he released Weezing, his Poison Pokémon.

Iron Mask pulled an unusual metallic black ball from his belt. He hurled it into the air and released a gigantic green fire-breathing Pokémon.

"What's that?" Misty cried.

"A Tyranitar," Brock stated. "But there's something funny about it."

"Destroy!" commanded Iron Mask.

Tyranitar opened its mouth to reveal a round orb of light. Suddenly, the orb transformed into a scorching flash of fire that sent Ash and his friends running for cover.

Tyranitar continued its fiery hot blasts as Iron Mask laughed.

"Two can play the Celebi stealing game," Jessie exclaimed. She ordered Weezing into battle. The purple Poison Pokémon let out a big bellowing puff of smoke.

"Who are you three?" Iron Mask demanded from his lofty perch.

Jessie, James, and Meowth suddenly realized who the mysterious villain was.

"The Iron-Mask Marauder!" they cried in unison.

"So you've heard about me!" Iron Mask smiled nastily.

"As you can tell from the uniforms," James said trying to impress Iron Mask, "we're also members of Team Rocket."

As Jessie and James tried to win the approval of Iron Mask, Ash and his friends ran away as fast as they could.

Iron Mask threw two more Poké Balls into the sky and sent Scizor and Sneasal after Celebi.

Chapter Five
Teamwork

"**M**isty!" Brock shouted as his friend stumbled and fell on the hard rocky ground.

"Ash!" Sammy shouted. "I think Misty's hurt!"

"I twisted my knee," Misty stammered, clutching her leg.

Ash hurried to Misty. "You better rest," he said.

"*Pika!*" cried Ash's Pokémon.

Ash looked up in concern. "Something's coming," he said just as Iron Mask's two nasty Pokémon appeared only a few feet away.

"They must want Celebi!" Brock exclaimed as he eyed the red stealy Scizor and the mean furry Sneasal.

"Then they're in for a battle," Ash declared.

Sammy carefully handed Celebi to Brock and pulled out a very old-fashioned Poké Ball. "I'm with you," he told Ash as he released a Charmeleon from the ball. It burst forth throwing scorching flames of fire.

Ash threw his own Poké Ball into the air. "Go!" he cried. A bright yellow Bayleef appeared. Instantly, Bayleef attacked Scizor with razor-sharp leaf blades. Both Pokémon flew through the air with blinding speed.

"Use your Vine Whip!" Ash shouted to his Pokémon.

Bayleef tried to obey, but Scizor divided its image. Bayleef was confused as hundreds of Scizors floated above the rock boulders.

Sneasal and Charmeleon raced around the multiple Scizor doing battle as Bayleef tried to hit its target. Bayleef began to look weak with confusion.

"Ash!" called Sammy. "Only one of them is real. Don't be fooled!"

"Bayleef." Ash spoke calmly but firmly. "Listen. Concentrate. You can find the right one."

Bayleef squinted its eyes and focused in on the Scizor. It waited until one image appeared stronger than the rest. Then it fired its strong, fierce Vine Whip. The Scizor fell, and the images disappeared.

"You did it!" shouted Ash. "Yeah, Bayleef!"

"You're a great trainer!" Sammy said with respect.

"It helps when you have a great Poké-mon." Ash smiled. But the victory was short-lived. All of a sudden Sneasal leaped forth.

"Charmeleon!" Sammy cried. "Use Head-butt!"

The dragonlike Pokémon did as it was told, and with one swift slam, it defeated Iron Mask's Sneasal.

"You're not a bad trainer yourself!" Ash exclaimed.

"We make a good team," Sammy agreed.

Ash looked at his Pokémon and then at Sammy. There was nothing better than Pokémon and friends.

But there was no time to enjoy their victory. They had to keep moving. The huge spider-legged metal machine was moving through the forest again. And now it was carrying more than just Iron Mask. Jessie, James, and Meowth were now on board, too. It didn't take long for them to discover their Pokémon laying defeated on the forest floor.

"Those kids aren't as wimpy as I thought they'd be," Iron Mask uttered. Then he hissed, "This makes things interesting."

Deep in the forest lives a mysterious time-traveling Pokémon named Celebi.

Forty years ago, Celebi was chased
by a Pokémon hunter.

Houndoom is all fired up.

To escape, Celebi blasts into the
future with Sammy.

Out of danger, but hurt and scared, Celebi hides in the bushes.

The kids race to the Lake of Life to heal Celebi's wounds.

Once in the lake,
Celebi is healed.

But Team Rocket and Meowth are never far behind.
They plot to steal the time-traveling Pokémon.

**Oh no!
Iron Mask has
captured
Celebi.**

Now the Pokémon is evil!

Not so fast, Iron Mask! Ash, Pikachu, and
Suicune are hot on your trail.

Suicune to the rescue!

Ash tries to free Celebi from
Iron Mask's evil clutches.

Hurray! With help from Suicune,
Ash and Pikachu save Celebi.

Ash and Pikachu have won their toughest battle yet

Chapter Six

The Lake of Life

Celebi lay panting in Sammy's arms.

"This is getting bad," Brock said quietly as he looked at the weak little Pokémon.

A thick fog had surrounded them. It wasn't clear which way to go.

"We better keep moving," Ash said solemnly. "We might be too late if we wait."

Then from out of the mist, two bearlike Pokémon appeared in their path.

"It's an Ursaring," Sammy said, gesturing to the very tall bear with a circle on its belly. A small fuzzy bear, a Teddiursa, stood at its side. They stared at Ash and Sammy.

"What're they doing?" Brock whispered.

"I think they're telling us to follow them," Misty said.

"Should we?" Ash questioned.

Sammy nodded. "Yeah."

The group of friends quietly followed the silent bearlike Pokémon through the mysterious forest. After they had walked a long way, a Stantler approached the Ursaring. Ursaring stepped back, and the deerlike Stantleer became the guide. The thick fog made it impossible to know where they were going. But they had to trust their Pokémon guide.

After several more miles, a little Furret took over for the Stantler. It ran ahead of the group but it popped in and out of the tall grass, always checking that the group was following.

Finally, after many hours of walking, Ash could see a clearing ahead. Then through the fog, a beautiful still wilderness lake appeared.

"Do you think this could be the Lake of Life that Diana's grandmother talked about?" Brock asked softly.

Celebi seemed nearly unconscious as Sammy waded into the lake. Sammy cradled the Pokémon in both arms and continued walking until the water was up to his chest. At first, it didn't seem to affect Celebi. It looked as though the sweet Pokémon might just slip away.

"Look!" Ash whispered in awe.

On the other shore, all the Pokémon of the forest had gathered. Hundreds of different kinds stood quietly side by side. They watched in hope as Celebi began to feel the power of the water. Suddenly, Celebi used its last bit of energy to push itself out of Sammy's arms and disappear into the deep waters. Everything was completely still. It was as if the world was waiting to see if Celebi would ever return.

Then something began to glow. Out in the lake, a circle of green light rose to the surface.

"This must be the Lake of Life," Brock said with hope. "The water must've brought Celebi back to life!"

As if on cue, Celebi exploded from the water. It soared into the sky, filling the air with the joyous ring of its playful sound. Ash and Sammy laughed as Celebi darted around them. The Pokémon of the forest watched happily as Ash and Sammy dove into the waters to swim with Celebi. They followed the Pokémon deep into the water where they were surrounded by strange and beautiful Water Pokémon. But Ash and Sammy could not stay underwater as long as Celebi. Soon they were struggling to the surface for air. Celebi raced after them and surrounded them with a white glowing outline.

When they hit the surface of the water, they kept going. Ash and Sammy were flying above the lake with Celebi. Ash couldn't believe it. What an incredible feeling! Down below they could see Misty and Brock smiling and waving. Ash had never felt so wonderful. For the rest of the day, Celebi led Ash and his friends on an amazing tour of the forest that ended at a tree with the reddest, ripest, sweetest berries any of them had ever tasted.

"These are really good," Ash exclaimed.

"They're delicious," Misty said as she popped a handful in her mouth.

As the day came to an end, Ash, Sammy, and Celebi climbed into the tree and watched the sunset.

Chapter Seven

Timeless Friends

Ash stirred from a deep sleep. He was curled into his sleeping bag next to the campfire. He opened his eyes and saw Sammy sitting up with a book in his lap.

"Sammy," Ash croaked, "it's the middle of the night."

"I can't sleep," Sammy replied as he continued to sketch in his book.

Ash sat up and looked at Sammy's drawings. The book was filled with beautiful pencil drawings of Pokémon.

"These are amazing!" Ash extolled. "It's like a handmade Pokédex." Sammy looked at him puzzled. "That's a machine that has pictures of Pokémon," Ash quickly explained.

"I guess you know a lot about the future . . . at least more than I do." Sammy said looking up at the star-filled sky.

Ash studied his new friend's face. He seemed sad.

"I think I'll like living in the future," Sammy said quietly, "but then I think about my mother worrying about me and wondering where I am. And I wonder if she still wonders." He was silent for a minute and then he turned to Ash. "What about your mom? Does she worry about you when you're out on your Pokémon Journey?"

"Yeah," Ash said, suddenly feeling a little sad himself. "I guess. Maybe that's just what moms do."

The two boys stood side by side in the light of the fire until Ash's stomach let out a loud growl. Sammy chuckled.

"Thinking about my mom gets me thinking about her cooking," Ash laughed.

Sam's face lit up. "Hey! I have something." He pulled a carefully wrapped loaf of bread from his bag. It was the one Diana's grandmother had given him — forty years ago. "Still looks pretty fresh!" Sammy laughed as he handed a piece to Ash.

The boys each took a bite.

"Great!" Ash exclaimed.

"Like it was made yesterday!" Sammy agreed.

A few feet away, Pikachu awoke from a curled sleep next to Celebi.

"*Pika*?" The Electric Pokémon got up and moved past the campfire.

"What's wrong, Pikachu?" Ash asked.

Pikachu led them to the edge of the clearing where they saw an incredible sight. Throughout the trees, small bursts of light radiated into the darkness. Ash and Sammy looked on in awe as a flock of Butterfree began to take wing. They filled the night sky with their glittering glow and their warbling call.

"Butterfree!" Sammy exclaimed.

"I hope you'll be free," Ash said to Sammy.

"Huh?" Sammy answered, confused by Ash's statement.

"To go back in time."

The two friends watched the night sky as the stars and Butterfree took turns filling it with light.

A beautiful clear blue-skied morning was waiting for them when they woke up. The crew packed up their camp and hurried to get on their way. Ash couldn't wait to see what else the amazing Celebi might show them today.

The group hiked happily through the forest as Celebi flitted around them in the air. Without warning, a long metal claw reached out from the forest trees and grabbed for Celebi.

Ash, Brock, Misty, and Sammy were surrounded, and Iron Mask and Team Rocket were inches from Celebi.

Chapter Eight

The Dark Side of Celebi

Thunderbolt!

Pikachu threw everything it had into attacking Iron Mask's big spider-legged machine. But it had no effect. The machine stepped into the clearing swinging its long legs through the forest growth. It cut down enormous old trees and destroyed everything in its path. Celebi had nowhere to hide. Iron Mask's laughter rang out loudly above the chaos.

Then a red basket at the end of a long arm reached out from the evil machine. It whipped through the madness and grabbed Celebi. The Pokémon was locked in its grip!

"Celebi!" Sammy cried.

Celebi was struggling wildly to free itself.

"This ought to calm you down," roared Iron Mask. He threw a switch, and Celebi's cage lit up with an electric shock. When it stopped, Celebi was stunned and still. Iron Mask grabbed the limp Pokémon and threw it into the air followed by a Dark Ball. Sammy and Ash watched in horror as Celebi disappeared into the terrible Dark Ball.

"Celebi is mine," boasted Iron Mask.

Ash never felt so angry. He let out a war cry and hurled himself toward the machine. He scaled the long legs up to where Iron Mask held Celebi in the Dark Ball.

"Stupid kids," hissed Iron Mask. All at once a flock of Pidgeys swooped down and attacked him.

By this time Ash had reached the platform and leaped onto Iron Mask's back. Iron Mask tried to throw him off, but Ash held strong. During the struggle Iron Mask knocked into the control panel, and the machine began to swerve and weave through the forest. Finally, it lurched so far that Ash went flying through the air and landed on the hard ground. He was in serious pain but he held the Dark Ball with all his might.

"He won't get you," Ash uttered to Celebi.

"I think that belongs to me," Iron Mask roared. His huge booted foot came down hard on Ash's hand. Ash fought not to give in to the pain. But Iron Mask pressed harder and harder, crushing Ash's fingers between the Dark Ball and his boot.

Ash held on until the pain became so great that he fell unconscious. Iron Mask quickly grabbed Celebi.

"Ash!" Sammy cried. The Pokémon of the forest gathered along with Ash's friends. They looked at Ash lying still and then they turned to Iron Mask.

"Don't waste your time," Iron Mask sneered. "It's too late for Celebi. The sweet little Pokémon you used to know doesn't exist anymore. See for yourself."

He hurled the Dark Ball into the air and called, "Celebi! Get rid of them all."

Celebi appeared from within the Ball. It

hung in midair as it formed a rippling energy field. Within a second or two, that energy field screamed through the air. It slammed everything in its path. Some Pokémon went flying backward. Those that could, ran for their lives.

Sammy could only cover his eyes as the little Pokémon destroyed the forest it was supposed to protect.

"You learn fast, Celebi," Iron Mask thundered. "Show me more!"

Celebi began to send energy blasts in every direction. The air filled with dirt and debris. The branches and wood from the destroyed forest began to swirl in the air. Celebi used more and more of its power to lift every bit of wood off the ground and spin it in a wild circle around itself. The wood spun faster and faster until it formed a nest that seemed nearly alive. Celebi hid itself away in the center of the creation. The nest continued to spin, creating its own life force. Its pull was so strong that Jessie was swept up into the air and disappeared inside.

Off in the distance, Diana and Towa

could see the top of the strange brown orb as it moved through the forest.

"What is that?" Diana asked nervously.

"I don't know," Towa answered. "Let's go see."

Chapter Nine

Iron Mask Rules

"Celebi!" Ash cried out as he sat up in pain.

"Take it easy," Misty said with a hand on Ash's shoulder. "You might be hurt!"

Iron Mask and Celebi's nest had disappeared from view. Ash was so confused. How could such a wonderful Pokémon be turned so bad so quickly?

Togepi let out a peep as White's boatplane flew toward them from the village.

"Stay right where you are!" Diana called from above.

"We're coming to get you," Towa shouted. When they were safely in the flying boat,

White lifted them back into the sky. It was painful to see Iron Mask's destructive path from above. It was impossible to believe he had used Celebi to do it.

Diana and Towa shook their heads in sadness. Towa said, "Forcing the spirit of the forest to destroy the forest. It's just despicable."

On the ground, the nest moved quickly, destroying everything it touched. Iron Mask was perched high atop it. He no longer needed his spider-legged machine. Celebi's nest was much more powerful.

Just inside it, Jessie hung upside down, tangled in a mess of thick green vines. "Could you let me out of here?" she whined to Iron Mask.

"Not yet," he barked. "I need a witness to report back to Giovanni. I want the head of Team Rocket to know just how powerful Celebi is . . . and how powerful I am! Celebi! Destroy!"

Deep in the center of the nest, Celebi began to radiate energy. The nest began to transform into something even more terrifying. Long arm extensions stretched out from the center, and legs began to appear. The round nest slowly became a horrible creature towering over the trees.

The nest creature turned toward the lake. It lowered its head slightly and sent a huge and powerful laser blast right into the water. Instantly, the lake appeared to die. Everything seemed to fade.

"With Celebi, I can rule Team Rocket and the whole world if I want to!" Iron Mask declared, and his terrible laugh rang throughout the forest. Jessie clung to the vines, terrified for her life.

From White's boat, Ash and the gang got a good view of the nest creature.

"What is that?" Towa shuddered.

"The evil Celebi must have created it," Brock answered.

White flew in to get a better look.

"Celebi," Ash cried when they were closer. He desperately wanted to reclaim the sweet Celebi. Everyone joined in, calling for Celebi, hoping to remind it of its kindness.

"You're annoying me," Iron Mask spat. "Celebi! Get rid of them!"

Ash called out again, "Celebi!"

But Celebi didn't listen. It shot another

deadly laser blast toward the boat. It missed, but the power was enough to send the boat spinning out of control. White fought to steady the vessel, but the boat spiraled through the sky toward the dark waters.

As they hit the water, clinging to each other for their lives, the nest creature struck again. This time, the laser didn't miss. It hit the boat directly.

Chapter Ten
Inside the Creature

After the crashing explosion, there was silence. The dying lake lay still. There was no sign of life anywhere until White's voice rang out. "Is everybody okay?"

"I think so," Misty whispered.

"I'm still alive," Brock stated strongly.

"Me too," Sammy called.

"So am I," Ash announced.

Diana stood without trouble, but her grandmother was in worse shape.

"I'm alive," groaned Towa, "but just barely."

There was no time to recover. The creature was coming in huge hulking steps.

"Pikachu! Try a thunderbolt!" Ash commanded.

Pikachu fired, but it had no effect. Iron Mask simply jumped off the creature and onto a tree branch to avoid the bolt. And the creature had no reaction at all.

Iron Mask then shouted, "Celebi! Get rid of these children!"

Deep inside the twig creature, Celebi's eyes slowly opened. Glowing orbs of energy flew toward the little Pokémon as it gathered strength. The glow around the mouth of the creature grew brighter and brighter. Ash and Sammy watched in horror.

ZZZZAAAAAPPPPP!

A laser blast of incredible power exploded from the creature. A great ball of fire and destruction rose up right where Ash and Sammy had been standing. Their friends watched in horror until suddenly, Ash and Sammy flew across the sky on the back of Suicune.

The beautiful and powerful Pokémon had swept the two boys right out of danger. Its purple mane flew in the wind while two satiny ribbons trailed elegantly behind it.

"The North Wind saved them!" Towa gasped.

"Suicune!" White whispered in awe.

"You must have come to help us," Ash said to the Pokémon hero. "Take us to Celebi!"

"This is my chance to capture Suicune." Iron Mask's ugly voice rose up. "Tyranitar! Do it!"

The large green Pokémon appeared. It shot a streak of fire at Suicune but missed.

Brock threw a Poké Ball into the air. "Go Onix!" he cried.

His long, Rock Pokémon emerged, ready to battle Tyranitar. But Tyranitar easily lifted Onix into the air and hurled it to the ground.

As that battle continued, Suicune flew Ash and Sammy up to the head of the creature.

"Celebi!" Sammy called.

The boys struggled to see the little Pokémon nested deep within the twig creature.

On the ground, Onix rallied and defeated Tyranitar. But Iron Mask wouldn't give up.

"Playtime is over, children! Celebi! Get them!"

"Suicune!" Ash called on his new Pokémon friend.

Suicune blasted the creature, but it was no use. The creature reached out and snared Suicune in a vine-and-twig grip. As Suicune struggled to get free, Ash and Sammy were thrown from its back. The twig creature threw bolts of electricity through Suicune. Ash and Sammy reached out in mid-air to save themselves from crashing to the ground. Jessie's hand reached out and helped them to safety inside the creature.

"You have to be careful," Jessie said without her usual attitude. "Celebi's right above us."

Ash and Sammy took off toward Celebi.

"Hey!" shouted Jessie. "Get me out of here!"

As Ash and Sammy climbed closer toward Celebi, they called out to it.

"Celebi, you have to stop!"

"You're supposed to protect the forest, not destroy it!"

That's when Celebi came into view. It was the same green Pokémon except for the evil look in its eyes. Ash and Sammy stared at it.

"Celebi," Ash said reaching out.

ZZZZZAAAAPPPP!

Celebi wrapped the boys in a long electrical shock. Ash and Sammy screamed in pain as Celebi stared at them in confusion.

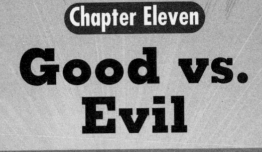

Chapter Eleven

Good vs. Evil

On the ground, Iron Mask was waiting for Celebi to destroy the boys. But instead of the attack getting stronger, Celebi was pulling back.

"What are you waiting for? They're our enemies!" Iron Mask shouted.

Celebi threw another wave of electricity around the boys, and Suicune. They writhed in pain.

"We're not your enemies," Ash gasped. "We want to save you."

For a split second, Celebi looked at Ash as if it remembered who he was.

"Try to remember," Ash encouraged.

"You brought me with you here to the future," Sammy reminded it.

"*Pika!*" Pikachu squeaked.

"Celebi, destroy them!" Iron Mask shouted.

Celebi began to thrash about. It struggled as Iron Mask's orders and its own memories battled each other in the Pokémon's mind.

Outside, the Pokémon of the forest had gathered. Their voices rose up and they begged Celebi to remember its good spirit.

Celebi screamed out in pain as its goodness fought the evil spell of Iron Mask's Dark Ball.

"Celebi," Sammy cried, "don't you remember?"

Ash and Sammy inched closer. They endured another blast of electricity but kept moving closer. Finally, Sammy was able to reach out and take Celebi in his arms. As he hugged the Pokémon, it threw waves of fiery current through him. But slowly, the evil was dying. Celebi's memories of Sammy and Ash brought the goodness inside it back to life.

Brock, Misty, White, Diana, and Towa

watched in wonder as the creature released Suicune. It stumbled into the lake and vanished into it. As it disappeared, Celebi surrounded the boys with its protective orb and flew Ash and Sammy to safety.

"We did it!" Ash cried joyfully.

On the other shore, Meowth and James saw Jessie land safely.

"Look!" James cried.

"Jessie!" Meowth screeched.

Ash's friends gathered at the lake's edge to wait for the trio to reappear.

"Ash is all right!" cried Misty.

"Yeah," Brock agreed. "And so is Sammy!"

"They've got Celebi, too," Towa added.

Their happy mood quickly quieted as Ash and Sammy walked out of the forest carrying a very still Celebi.

"What's wrong?" Misty uttered.

"I don't know," Ash whispered. "Something bad."

Chapter Twelve

From the Great Beyond

Celebi lay shriveled in Ash's arms. It no longer glowed green. It was ash gray.

"Get it to the water," Brock cried.

Ash bent down and covered Celebi in the lake water, but nothing happened.

"The forest is hurt. The water's tainted. The lake is . . . dying." Towa shook her head sadly.

From behind them, they heard the swish of Suicune.

"Suicune has the power to make the water clean again!"

Suicune took to the air and flew back

and forth across the water. It touched down again and again across the surface of the lake. Every time its hoof touched, a circle of bright blue life spread out across the water.

"The legend's true," White said.

"The North Wind saved the lake," Diana said in awe.

But no sooner did Suicune return to shore than the bright blue waters went black again. The destruction had been so great, it seemed even Suicune could not change it.

Ash lowered Celebi to the water again.

"It isn't working," Towa said in a hushed voice.

"We'll keep trying!" Ash cried desperately. He pulled berries from his pockets. "These are the berries we found in the forest." He tried to rouse Celebi, but there was no sign of life. Tears began to fall from his eyes.

"Celebi!" he suddenly shouted. "You can't die!"

Sammy's tears mixed with the water of the lake as he watched Celebi.

"Celebi didn't do anything wrong," he choked out. "It was a human being who forced Celebi to destroy the forest. Celebi never had a choice! And now Celebi's gonna die!"

A great wailing cry rose up from the forest as the Pokémon heard Sammy's voice. Suicune lifted its proud head and roared with an anguish that filled the forest.

As the sadness swallowed the forest, the sky began to radiate with a pulsating white light. The light grew into a circle as bright as the sun. As the humans and Pokémon looked toward the sky, it filled with Celebi, flown across time to collect their dying friend. Hundreds of Celebi flew noiselessly down from the light. They gently lifted Sammy's Celebi and flew back toward the light. The band of Celebi surrounded the dying Celebi. The sweet sound of their song filled the air.

Ash and Sammy watched as their Celebi was about to disappear. But then, Celebi's limp body jerked. Its eyes slowly opened. It let out a small trilling call.

Ash let out a cry of joy and relief.

Celebi pulled itself upright and flew back toward the ground. Its voice grew stronger as the forest began to radiate with good forces. The rescuing Celebi disappeared into the light as Sammy's Celebi flitted back and forth across the lake.

Ash and his friends cheered in celebration. Celebi flew inches above the water as it came straight toward Sammy. Celebi was back!

But as it neared the shore, Iron Mask burst up from beneath the water. In a blinding second, he held Celebi in his evil grip . . . again.

Chapter Thirteen

Homeward Bound

"**G**ive it back!" Ash screamed.

Iron Mask responded by firing up his jet pack and shooting into the sky. With Pikachu on his back, Ash grabbed onto Iron Mask's leg.

"Get off me, kid!" Iron Mask shouted. He kicked and jerked his legs as the trio soared higher.

"Pikachu!" Ash called. "Use Thunderbolt!"

Pikachu lit up the sky with its power. Iron Mask screamed in pain. His jet pack burned out, and he began to fall toward the ground. So did Ash and Pikachu.

"Pikachu!" Ash screamed as they fell faster and faster.

But suddenly they hung weightless, suspended in the air. From the ground, his friends could see Celebi's protective light glowing around Ash and Pikachu.

"Celebi!" Ash exclaimed in awe.

As Ash and Pikachu sailed gently down, Iron Mask crashed through the trees and landed with a thud. He rolled down a sloping rock and lay moaning on the ground.

Towa stood above him. "You tried to destroy the forest, and we don't take kindly to that kind of behavior."

The forest's Pokémon surrounded Iron Mask. He sat powerless and shaking. Now, none of his Pokémon would respond to his command.

"This is a mistake," he stuttered, "a big misunderstanding."

A group of Caterpie, Weedle, and Spinarak spit out hundreds of yards of silk string. They wound it around Iron Mask until he couldn't move a muscle.

"I think the Pokémon understand perfectly," Towa laughed.

Ash turned his attention to Suicune. The noble Pokémon stood silently among the trees of the forest.

"Thank you," Ash said.

Suicune stood for another moment before it turned and disappeared into the trees.

Celebi flitted by the group and up into the sky. Then it stopped to look at Sammy.

"Looks like Celebi's getting ready to travel back in time. And I think it wants to take you along, Sammy," Towa said.

Sammy looked in disbelief as Celebi began to glow.

"Looks like you're going home," Ash said with a mix of emotion.

"I guess so," Sammy answered softly.

"Don't worry," Ash told him. "No matter where you are or even *when* you are . . . we'll always be friends."

Sammy smiled as the spirit of Celebi began to lift him off the ground. The light across the sky danced through the forest. Ash's friends stood behind him and waved good-bye to Sammy.

"Thank you, Ash. You're a great friend. Maybe I'll see you again . . . *some* day!"

Sammy had nearly disappeared into the light as Ash waved back and shouted, "Some day we will!"